MARTHA SPEAKS

Martha Bakes a Cake

Adaptation by Karen Barss

Based on a TV series teleplay written by Raye Lankford

Based on the characters created by Susan Meddaugh

HOUGHTON MIFFLIN HARCOURT

Boston • New York • 2012

Ages 5–7 | Grade: 2 | Guided Reading Level: J | Reading Recovery Level: 17 | Lexile® Level: 380L

For information about permission to reproduce selections from this book, write to Permissions,
Houghton Mifflin Harcourt, 215 Park Avenue South, New York, NY 10003.
Library of Congress Cataloging-in-Publication Data is on file.

ISBN: 978-0-547-68113-9 paperback | ISBN: 978-0-547-68102-3 hardcover

Design by Rachel Newborn
www.hmhbooks.com | www.marthathetalkingdog.com
Manufactured in Singapore | TWP 10 9 8 7 6 5 4 3 2 1 | 4500343609

Helen is feeling down in the dumps.
Her drawing did not win the art contest.

"Your drawing was terrific," says Mom.
"You have to say that. You are my mom," says Helen.

Mom drops Helen off at school.

Mom wants to cheer up Helen.
At work, Mom has an idea.
"I know," she says. "I will bake her a cake!"

Licking the bowl
will cheer me up!

Just then the phone rings.

Mom gets a big order.
Now she does not have time to bake a cake
from scratch.

It's up to us, Skits!

Martha and Skits run home.
Martha pushes a button.
The TV turns on.

They watch Helen's baking DVD.

"First, collect your ingredients," says the TV cook.

"To start, you need eggs, milk, and butter."

Martha and Skits go into the kitchen.
Skits grabs a milk carton.
His teeth make holes and it leaks.

He takes it to the living room.
Skits drops it on the floor.

He goes back to the kitchen.
Skits grabs an egg carton.
He drops it next to the milk.

All the eggs crack!

Martha and Skits walk home holding the eggs.

A squirrel runs by as they near the door.
Both dogs drop their eggs to bark.

Oh, bummer.

Martha knows what to do.
"More eggs? What next? Flour? Milk?" asks
Mrs. Parkington.
"Now that you mention it," says Martha.

Thanks, again.

Mrs. Parkington puts everything in a wagon.
Then she pulls the wagon to Martha's house so
the ingredients do not spill.

Then Martha and Skits get to work.
"Pour the ingredients into a bowl," says the TV cook. "Stir well."

Martha wants to pour the flour into her dog dish.
She spills it all over.

"Let's just mix everything here on the rug," says Martha.

So Martha and Skits pour out all the ingredients.

They blend them together with their paws.
Then they push the batter into Martha's bowl.

"Looking good!" says Martha.

Martha and Skits get the batter into the pan.

We did it!

The dogs are covered with flour.
They shake it off.
Then they push the cake pan into the kitchen.
But how will Martha and Skits bake the cake?

We can't turn on the oven!

Luckily, Howie the mailman comes to the door.
"Howie," says Martha, "can you help us?"

Martha asks Howie to turn on the oven and
put in the cake.
After Howie leaves, Martha says, "In thirty
minutes, we take out the cake."

Then Martha calls Wagstaff City Pizza. "Can you deliver a pizza in thirty minutes?" she asks.

When the pizza delivery boy comes, Martha asks him to take out the cake.

Just in time.

Just then, Helen and Mom come home.

Surprise!

"We baked you a cake to cheer you up!" cries
Martha.

Dad comes in. "Who wants cake?" he asks.

"What if I eat Dad's cake," asks
Helen, "and keep yours forever?"

"That would be a waste of cake," says Martha.
Skits barks.
"Great idea, Skits," says Martha.